*Ties of the Past*
*Western MF Romance Story*
**Author: Cathy Marshall**



**From the Author:**
Thank you for purchasing this book.

# Table of Contents


**Ties of the Past** ........................................................ 3

**Description** .............................................................. 3

**Chapter 1** ............................................................... 4

**Chapter 2** ............................................................... 7

**Chapter 3** ............................................................. 10

**Chapter 4** ............................................................. 12

**Chapter 5** ............................................................. 16

**Chapter 6** ............................................................. 20

**Chapter 7** ............................................................. 27

**Chapter 8** ............................................................. 40

**Chapter 9** ............................................................. 45

Kylie Stevens and Wade Collins were childhood best friends turned into lovers when fate played a trick on them and drew them apart and Kylie moved away causing Wade to be heartbroken.

Twelve years later, Kylie is back in town for her uncle's burial. She runs into Wade who doesn't want anything to do with the girl who broke his heart years ago.

Kylie is keen on rekindling their friendship while Wade wants nothing to do with her.

Would Wade ever open his heart and listen to the reason Kylie broke his heart years ago or would he continue to push her away?

Would Kylie take the secret to her grave with Wade seemingly married with a daughter?

Would fate succeed in pulling them apart yet again or finally bring them together?

It all lies in the Ties of the Past...

Chapter 1

Twenty-eight-year-old, Kylie Stevens dressed in a black gown stood in front of her Uncle's grave situated in the ranch's backyard.

The ranch was filled up with people from neighboring ranches and she could hear some of the people wailing making her to scoff inwardly.

Her uncle, Rhye Stevens was one of Georgia's most successful ranchers but he was known to be ruthless and heartless as well.

Everyone hated him because he treated people below him like shit and stepped on people in order to get to the top.

If they were crying, it was just for eye-service. Most of the people present were there out of curiosity and others for the refreshments.

She could feel people's stares boring into her. She couldn't blame them though.

She had just flown in few days ago from the United States just in time for the burial.

She hadn't stepped in the country in years and was surprised that they could even recognise her.

She fixed her sunglasses staring down at her uncle's grave.

He had not only been cruel to outsiders but to her as well. He was the reason she was an orphan from the day she was born.

Her uncle had resented her father for being poor and tried to break his relationship with her mother.

It caused the two lovers to elope with their car getting into an accident and her father dying on the spot. Her heavily pregnant mom went into premature labor and died after giving birth to her.

If her uncle had tried to make it up to her parents by taking her in, he didn't show it.

He didn't miss the chance to taunt her every time for being the cause of her mother's death and the result of an ill-fated love.

He was also the reason she had to leave Georgia to an unknown country all by herself to start a new life.

She had vowed not to step into Georgia until his death. She didn't want to see the man who ruined her life due to his greed and arrogance.

Given a choice, she wouldn't have come back due to the horrid memories she witnessed in that ranch courtesy of his cruel actions but as the only living relative, it was her job to entertain the guests.

Her eyes flicked through the guests until she caught a glimpse of a tall man with a Stetson hat on who looked familiar, standing several feet away.

"Is that who I think it is?" She thought to herself trying to place his face but the people before him were blocking him from her view.

"Kylie." She heard the familiar voice of her nanny, Sara, call her name.

Kylie turned to look at her worried nanny.

"Are you okay, what were you staring at?"

"No one in particular." She hated lying to her precious Nanny but she was not ready to dwell on that topic yet.

"If you say so. Here take this."

She handed Kylie a cup filled with orange juice and the latter smiled in gratitude at her heartfelt gesture.

"You still remember my favorite juice."

She shrugged. "How could I ever forget my baby's favorite drink?"

Kylie embraced the only woman she knew as her mother, letting her body relax in her arms.

The funeral preparations had taken a toll on both of them.

It felt nice knowing that she still had someone who loves her and cares for her.

She patted Kylie's back lovingly and pulled out of the hug.

She tugged a stray hair disturbing your vision behind your ear.

''I will be over there attending to the guests in case you need me.''

Kylie nodded glad that she still had a pillar of support.

Sara excused herself while Kylie looked behind her in search of the familiar face but he seemed nowhere to be found.

Kylie sighed and face palmed herself thinking to herself that she might have imagined him.

Wade would never step foot in the ranch of his worst enemy, her uncle, especially not after what the latter put him through.

She surely imagined it. she shook her head blaming the stress for her imagination and went on greeting every visitor.

Chapter 2

Wade Collins dismounted from his favorite black Stallion on getting to the Stevens Ranch.

Removing his hat, he wiped the sweat from his brow caused by the scorching sun beating down on him.

He put his hand on his waist and looked around amazed at the large number of people at the funeral.

Rhye Stevens was the cruelest that ever existed in Georgia.

The people were surely not there for him but to make sure that he was dead and to relish in the delicacy which he would have denied them if he were alive.

They were there to have the last laugh.

Wade Collins brushed his brown hair back and sighed.

If not for Katherine, he wouldn't have even bothered coming to the funeral. He hated Rhye Stevens with every drop of his blood and the feeling was mutual.

The man had made his life a living hell just because of his poor status and the fact that he fell in love with his niece.

The heartless man had subjected him to several beatings and cold tortured nights just because of a love that was not worth it.

''Wade you are here?'' Frank Fisher, the owner of the fisher ranch down the road stated in surprise as he walked up to Wade.

The latter let out the breath, he didn't know he was holding and nodded. ''Yeah, I just came to check on my property.''

It was partly true. He hadn't come to pay his last respects to the dead man. He owed him no respects and he was dead sure that the dead asshole wouldn't want that either.

He was just there to make sure that his share of the Ranch was not damaged during the burial. He wasn't about to go easy on anybody who tried to ruin it.

Frank Fisher nodded. ''I guessed as much given that you were both sworn enemies.''

''You know his niece is back in town for the funeral.''

Wade's ear picked up at the mention of Rhye's niece. He frowned ''She's here?''

Frank Fisher nodded and pointed to where several people were standing. ''She's right in front of his grave.''

Against his better judgement, Wade's eyes followed his direction and he ended up straining his eyes until; he caught a glimpse of a fair head woman talking to Nanny Sara.

He could only see her side profile but there was no mistaking that it was Kylie, his first love.

His heart picked up race beating at a frantic rate as he stared at the woman who broke his heart years ago.

''We all thought she wouldn't come back but alas, it took her uncle's death to bring her back from the states.''

Frank's word cut through his thoughts.

It was true. This was the first time he would set his eyes on her after twelve years. From what he could see from where he was standing, her cheek bones were more pronounced, she seemed to have lost the baby fat on her cheeks.

''I wouldn't blame her for not coming back, If I ever went to the states, I won't come back ether, you know.''

Wade felt his anger build in him at Frank's last statement. He didn't even know why he came there anymore. He just needed to leave as soon as possible.

Seeing Kylie again brought back sweet and sad memories he had tried to bury with her departure years ago but had failed to.

She had chosen a new life over their love, humiliated him when she was the only one he could trust and now she had the audacity to come back and wreak havoc to the indifference he had built up for years.

"I have to go."

Frank scrunched up his eyebrow in confusion. "But you just got here."

Wade didn't have time for chit chats. No one knew about his love history with Kylie.

They just knew that they were best friends, nobody knew about their secret rendezvous and it was better if it stayed that way.

He mounted his house and galloped out of the ranch mentally beating himself up for even showing up there.

Deep down in his sub-conscious, wade knew that he had only come to the burial for her and her only.

# Chapter 3

Later that night, Wade tossed and turned trying to get some sleep but he knew he wouldn't be falling asleep easily especially when a certain woman plagued his mind all day.

He would be lying if he said he hadn't given much thought to the fact that Kylie would be home for her uncle's burial. He expected it and that was the driving force to him attending the ceremony even though he hated to admit it even to himself.

Even though she had broken his heart years ago, his heart still only beat for her. She had made him distrustful of women and he had wanted nothing to do with them.

Just when he thought his life was in order, she just had to show up and mess up the indifference he had been building for years.

He drank with his peers after a long time just to get her face out of his system and now he was suffering the aftermath.

He remembered the time he had confessed his love to her at an abandoned building with sunflowers, her favorite flowers and how happy she had been jumping into his arms and declaring that she had been waiting for him to confess.

They kept their relationship a secret from her uncle who hated his guts and made his life a living hell for even hanging out with her. He still had the scars from the beatings he endured form the hands of her uncle.

It was six months into their relationship when they shared a heated kiss and made love in the barn. It was messy with neither of them having done that before but it was an exhilarating experience.

It was during one of their intimate sessions that her uncle had caught them and had him beaten and thrown into a cold dark room where he was kept for a week with no food, water or sunlight.

That didn't stop them from meeting behind her uncle's back. Nothing in the world could stop them so he thought until she decided to break things off in the most-cruel way possible.

She had used him as an experiment and discarded him like waste when she was bored with him.

He had suffered for nothing in the name of love.

After her, he vowed not to have any kind of relationship with another woman, whether serious or a fling. She had broken his heart beyond repair and he couldn't trust her kind anymore.

Now that she was in town, he wondered if he could keep up with the indifference he had mastered over the years in case they meet.

In fact given the circumstances he had roped himself in, they would have no choice but to interact for the sake of their equal share in the ranch.

Perhaps, she won't be interested in running it and offer to sell it to him instead.

He soon drifted off to sleep dreaming of a fair headed damsel clad in a black gown staring at him with her gorgeous emerald eyes.

Chapter 4

Kylie had just finished her early morning run when she turned round the corner and saw the infamous mercantile shop of Mrs. Aubrey.

She smiled as memories of her playing hide and seek in the shop with Wade flashed through her mind in a flash.

She started for the shop wanting to see if it was still owned by the nice Mrs. Aubrey.

In her haste to get inside the Shop, she bumped into the hard chest of a tall man who was just on his way out of the store.

''I'm sorry, are you ok?''

She heard the familiar deep but husky voice ring in her ears as the man helped her straighten up.

She looked up in time to behold his shocked face. Alas, it was Wade in flesh.

''Wade?'' She called, her voice barely a whisper. It was as if she had to make sure he was there in front of her and not a dream.

She couldn't help but stare and memorize each part of him. He looked even more handsome and muscular than before.

The fact that the first few buttons of his chest were open didn't help matters at all, it only caused butterflies to dance around her stomach.

Wade's mouth opened slightly in shock as he took in the mature face of his first love.

Her blonde hair was packed up in a messy bun with little or no makeup on her face yet she looked absolutely stunning.

She stared back at him with those piercing green eyes that always made him weak in the knee every time he stared at them.

His eyes swept over her form like a map he had to memorize in seconds.

She was wearing a tank top over light blue jeans. The top fit her perfectly. She had filled up nicely beyond his wildest dreams.

She had the face of an angel and a body that invited sin. He felt a stirring go through him as his pulse quickened.

Then the memory of the torture he suffered in the hand of her uncle and the way she trampled on his self-esteem flashed before his eyes and he stiffened giving her a cold glare.

"Do I know you?"

His question took her by surprise leaving her speechless. She wondered if he didn't recognise her. She could have sworn that he did a few moments ago.

"I thought as much." He fixed his sunglasses and brushed past her like she was nothing.

Finally finding her voice, she called after him.

"Wade, it's me Kylie. Your childhood best friend." She explained believing that he didn't recognise her and ignoring the fact that it hurt that he didn't.

He scoffed and turned to look at her. "I don't know anybody who goes by that name and it would be better for you to honour your part of the agreement."

He walked off leaving her confused by his statement.

It took her few minutes before she got the secret meaning in his message.

She had told him twelve years ago, when he came to beg her not to leave, that it was better that they acted like they didn't know each other.

Even after several years had passed, he still honored the agreement.

"Are you buying anything, my pretty lady?" Mrs. Aubrey cut through her thoughts and she looked up to meet her eyes through the window.

Your heart leapt with joy on seeing the woman who now had grey stands of hair displaying her old age.

"Yes."

Kylie walked into the shop and stood in front of the counter, beaming.

"Mrs. Aubrey, don't you recognise my face. It's me, Kylie."

She frowned and fixed her glasses on the rim of her nose before realization flashed before her eyes.

"Kylie!" She screamed and left the counter, pulling you into a heart-warming hug, swaying you in her arms.

She released you from the hug, her hand still holding onto your shoulder while she scanned your face.

"I can't believe that you are right here, standing in front of me, when did you come back?"

"Two days ago, I came back for the burial."

Her smile drops. "Oh! I'm sorry for your loss."

Kylie chuckled. "No, you are not sorry. Nobody is."

The woman joined him in laughing. "Good riddance."

Somehow Kylie felt bad making fun of the dead but she couldn't help herself.

Mrs. Aubrey sat you on the bench outside her store and held her hand in hers.

"Did you see Wade when you walked in?"

Kylie shook her head choosing not to draw unnecessary attention to her hopeless situation with Wade.

''I remember when the two of you used to run around playing in my store. Those were the good old days. I always teased you  that you two would end up together.''

Kylie smiled reminiscing on those days when she and Wade were as tight as thieves.

Wade's Mother was a worker at her Uncle's ranch and Wade used to accompany his mother to work every time.

Kylie, then six was trying to catch a butterfly when she saw a boy her age climbing up her uncle's tree.

She watched in amazement as the cute boy sat on the tree and he held his hand out for her to take.

 She didn't know why she trusted him that day but she held unto his hand and he sat her up the tree beside him and that started a short-lived friendship and romance, the latter was a secret to outsiders.

Her heart sank as she remembered the cold look he gave her.

She knew she deserved it for turning her back on him when he needed her the most.

She just hoped she would get a chance to tell him her side of the story. Maybe, just maybe, they could be cordial.

Chapter 5

''Given the fact that half of the ranch belongs to someone else, your uncle has given you total control over his share of the ranch and his finances.'' Lawyer Calvin said as he closed the will he was reading and looked at Kylie.

''He sold half of the ranch?'' Kylie asked in surprise.

Her uncle would never sell the ranch, he loved it too much to do that. It helped fuel his ego.

Lawyer Calvin nodded. ''He did. He had no choice and was put in a tight spot. He was on the verge of losing the ranch and he had to sell half his share to survive.''

''How come he never told me this?''

Lawyer Calvin shrugged. ''He obviously didn't want to worry you.''

Kylie frowned. She had stopped collecting allowances from her Uncle when she turned eighteen and had worked odd jobs just to be independent and free from his tyranny.

She couldn't care less about the ranch or her uncle so it made sense why he never told her about it.

"Who owns the half?" She asked as she sipped her drink savoring its taste in her mouth.

"One Wade Collins."

She sat up in shock wondering if he had heard him right ''Excuse me, what did you say his name is again?''

The lawyer stared at you confusedly probably wondering why you were acting strange.

''Wade Collins.'' He repeated.

She gasped wondering how that was possible. How could Wade be able to buy half the share and why did her uncle allow the man he loathed to buy it.

Those were pending questions plaguing her mind and she knew that there was only one person who could give answers to them and it was none other than Sara.

She excused herself from the Lawyer and made sure that the maids attended to his needs before making her way to Sara's room.

Millions of questions ran through her mind.

On getting to Sara's room, she knocked on the door.

''Sara, it's Kylie, I need to talk to you about something important.''

She heard a faint "come in" and entered to see Sara arranging her clothes into her wardrobe.

''What is it, you look troubled?''

''I just heard from the lawyer that my uncle sold half the ranch not just to anybody but to Wade of all people.''

''Do you know why he did that and where did Wade get the money to pay him.''

Sara sighed and sat on the bed facing Kylie.

''A year after you left, a family friend of the Collins came over to their house and stated that their old madam was dying and had willed her entire wealth to Wade due to the fact that she didn't have any child of her own."

''Wade was able to use the money wisely. He currently has a share in almost every ranch here. He's the now the richest ranch owner your uncle.''

The information surprised and pleased her as well. She felt so proud of Wade, all his dreams had come true just like he had envisioned but one thing was still not clear to her.

''But why did my uncle sell it to him, we both know that they hate each other's guts.''

''Well, nobody was willing to help your uncle out of his debt because of his wicked ways but Wade stepped in and cleared the debt, in return he was given the share of the property."

"Wow!" Kylie exclaimed in surprise. Wade had the opportunity to buy off the whole ranch but he settled for just half of it.

It didn't seem like revenge to her, he obviously had another reason which she couldn't grasp at that moment.

''Don't you think it's time to tell Wade the truth.''

''He hates me.''

Sara held your right hand in hers ''I don't think so. He's just angry but he would get over it when he learns the truth.''

''I saw him today and he said I shouldn't act like I know him. I'm sure if I go there he would send me away.''

''But you wouldn't know until you try right? The Kylie I know doesn't give up and I know you are not about to right now.''

She was right. Even though, it had been twelve years since she had seen Wade, her love for him had never died. It had only grown stronger.

She found herself thinking of him every time her friends set her up on a blind date against her wish. It led to a point where they just gave up on her and she buried her head in her books and work too emotionally unavailable.

No other man could make her heartbeat like Wade. She just hoped he still felt the same about her too.

''Ok I will go and see him now.''

''That's my girl and remember, melting his anger is not going to be easy just be patient.''

Kyle nodded ''I will. Thanks Nan.'' She embraced her.

''You are welcome, little one.''

After Sara gave her the address of Wade's Ranch, Kylie headed out to get her love back.

Chapter 6

To say she was nervous would be an understatement. She was anxious, excited and scared all at the same time.

The fact that she was standing in front of his Ranch didn't help matters either.

She considered leaving and coming back another day but she remembered her Nanny's words and decided against giving up.

Kylie breathed in and breathed out gathering enough courage before looking back up to behold the magnificent Ranch.

Wade had done well for himself and exceeded her expectations. His farm was large with large number of horses and cattle confined in the barn.

His ranch was obviously the biggest and his house was more beautiful and had a modern twist to it.

She felt out of place just standing by the wall observing the surroundings.

"Is something wrong?" A soft voice broke through her thoughts and she turned to behold a pretty woman with short black hair holding unto a cute little girl who didn't look to be past five years old.

The woman seemed to have come from inside the ranch and Kylie assumed that she worked there.

She smiled "No, there's nothing wrong. I'm just here to see the owner of the Ranch."

The woman smiled and brushed her stray hair away "You mean Wade?"

The little girl bounced up and down holding her candy as she giggled "That's my daddy."

Kylie felt her heart drop to her stomach at the little girl's words.

''Your daddy?''

The little girl nodded scrunching her eyes in order to be able to see Kylie face clearly due to the scorching sun ''He bought me this candy.''

''Sandy, that's enough.'' The woman scolded the little girl before looking up at Kylie.

She wanted to say something but was cut off by Wade who jogged over, looking as dashing as ever.

''What's going on here?'' he asked, his eyes fixed on you with a hard glare.

He had spotted her in front of his ranch and had excused himself from his men jogging over to see her.

Kylie could feel the tears spring up to her eyes as she stared at the three. The fact that Wade could be married or engaged hadn't crossed her mind. She was such a fool.

''This lady asked to see you.'' The woman pointed at Kylie who had been rendered speechless looking anywhere else but at the trio.

''Ok, you two can go back inside. I will take it up from here.'' Wade smiled at the woman and pecked her cheek. He then gave the little girl a kiss on the forehead an action which didn't go unnoticed by Kylie and only made her heart break the more.

The woman and her daughter went back inside while Wade buried his hands in his pants pocket and folded his arms.

''Care to tell me why you want to see me?''

Kylie couldn't bring herself to talk for fear that she would break down in front of him. She just needed to get out of there as fast as possible with the last thread of her dignity.

So she did the first thing her brain told her to do. She ran heading to no-where in particular but wanting to be far away from him as much as possible.

''Kylie!'' She heard him call her name but she didn't pay heed to him and continued on her mission to get away from him.

In her haste, she didn't notice a small rock and slipped on it causing her to land on her face to the dusty floor.

''Shit!'' He cursed from behind her and bent to her level helping her up.

''What is the matter with you?'' He scolded as he surveyed her body for any injuries.

Embarrassed, she took a step back not wanting him to touch her.

He raised his eyebrow in confusion and worry, when he saw her tear-filled eyes and closed the distance between them.

He brushed the stray tear away, the slight touch of his fingers on her cheek sent shivers down her spine and she took a step back, an action which didn't go unnoticed by him.

Hurt flashed in his eyes mistaking her actions towards him and he held her by the hand pulling her to him

''Does my presence disgust you now, If so, why then did you come to see me?''

Unable to control her tears now, they fell freely down her cheeks.

She had never felt so humiliated in her entire life. She was covered in dust, her joint and ankle were aching and she was sure she looked a mess and it didn't help matters that his hold on her was strong.

''Please just let me go.''

''You have to tell me why you had the audacity to come here after everything you did to me?'''

''Please, you are hurting me.'' She pleaded which snapped him out of his trance and he looked down at where he was holding her noticing the red mark there.

He quickly withdrew his hand as if he had been electrocuted and brushed his hair back feeling remorseful

''Oh my God! I'm sorry. I wasn't thinking.''

''You are hurt.'' He noted as he took in the bruises on her ankle that he hadn't seen in the first place.

Before Kylie could regain her composure and leave, he had carried her over his shoulder to her surprise.

''What are you doing?'' Her voice came out a s croak.

He shrugged heading towards his Ranch ''Taking you to get treatment for your wounds.''

''I'm fine. Just let me down.''

''Not on my watch!''

He ignored you as you hit his back and telling him to put you down as entered his ranch.

His workers were beginning to stare at them wondering who she probably was and why she was causing such a ruckus but she couldn't care less.

She just wanted him to put her down and let her go. Being in proximity with him was not helping her confused state.

He took her to the infirmary and told everyone to leave to her surprise leaving him alone with her.

He sat her on the bed and went about looking for the first aid kit. On spotting it by the drawer in the corner of the room, he took it out and went back to where she was seated meeting the teary eyes that haunted him.

He couldn't help but feel that he was at fault for making her feel that way.

He bent and took hold of her leg in order to apply ointment but she swatted his hand away.

"Don't touch me."

He chuckled mirthlessly. "You better sit still or I will confine you in here against your will."

His tone was warning and his eyes had a dangerous glint in them that showed her that he meant every word he uttered.

She bit her lower lip not knowing that the simple act was driving him insane.

She decided to let him have his way. She was after all too tired to fight back.

He cleaned off her wounds, applied the ointment as carefully as he could.

"Done!" he stated and looked up to meet her eyes.

She was staring at him in a strange way and he couldn't read her.

"What?" He asked as he stood up and wiped his hand with a hand towel.

Kylie shook her head and tried to step down from the bed but he stopped her.

"Wait!"

"What else does he want now?" She thought to herself.

"You need to change into something better." He opened the wardrobe at the corner of the room and brought out a short light blue dress.

"This is just like your size."

She stared at the cloth in his hand and right back up at him "Why are you being so nice to me? Won't your wife be worried when she sees me in her dress."

He frowned not getting her point "My wife?"

"Yeah, I'm sure no woman would take it kindly when they see a strange lady wearing her cloth that her husband had given to her."

"What are you talking about?" he was truly confused.

"The woman that I met at your ranch is your wife and that was your daughter beside her right?"

Realization flashed in his eyes as he got her point. He burst out into uncontrollable laughter startling her.

What she wouldn't admit was that his laughter was a pleasant sound to her ears.

"Just wear this." He handed her the dress still smiling trying to control his laughter.

"But-" She tried to protest.

"You are not a threat to her." He simply stated catching her off guard.

She felt like she had been kicked in the stomach.

He smirked as he studied her sad expression. "Are you by any chance jealous?"

She scoffed trying to preserve the last bit of her dignity "Of course not, why would I be?"

"Great! Because you have no right to be,"

He was right. She didn't have the right to feel betrayed or jealous. She had left him, what did she expect that he would be pining after her for the rest of his life?

"When you are done, get off my ranch"

He cast her a cold glare before leaving the infirmary.

She was surprised by his quick switch.

Wade stepped out and touched his chest feeling his heart beating frantically against it.

He had no choice but to get out of there as soon as possible before he did the unthinkable and kiss her.

He was letting his guard down and he didn't like that at all.

Chapter 7

Desperately in a need of fresh air, Kylie mounted her white stallion and galloped out of her ranch willing to forget her troubles.

She had found it hard to sleep the other night and had tossed and turned, crying her eyes out at her lost love.

Sara had tried to know what went wrong but she had locked herself in the room bawling her eyes out.

With dark circles under her eyes and a broken heart to mend, Kylie just needed a breather.

The horse was slow and unsteady on its feet to her disappointment.

''So much for getting a much-needed fresh air,'' She muttered under her breath.

''Ride em' cowgirl, yee-haw!'' yelled a teenage boy whom she passed by ignoring him.

Given no other choice in the matter, she had to pass by Wade's Ranch and against her better judgement, she looked at it.

She spotted him talking to one of his worker giving orders and he looked hot doing it. It didn't help matters that he was dressed in a pair of jeans and a blue long-sleeved shirt with the first three buttons open, showing his hard chest.

The man sure knew how to get attention.

Their eyes met and she quickly looked away. She had been caught checking a married man out and it made her feel sick and stupid at the same time.

Frustrated by her horse's slow speed, she mistakenly pulled at the reins and it suddenly started to move at an increasingly alarming rate.

''Slow down horse, slow down.'' She muttered panic evident in her voice.

She didn't know how to control it and it scared her at how fast it was moving. She came out for fresh air but in the end all she got was dust from the horse which gave her a coughing fit.

''Kylie, wait up, we need to talk.'' She heard Wade call from behind her.

She frowned wondering when he had gotten behind her and what else they had to talk about.

She was torn between being relieved that he was there or sad that the man she was running away from had caught up with her again.

Wade frowned when he saw that she wasn't slowing down. He tried to keep up with her speed and sidled up next to her.

''I must commend you for being such a speedy driver.''

''I'm not driving it, it's driving me. I've lost control over it.'' She gave a panicked reply while his eyes widened at her words.

''Calm down, I will fix this'' He assured her, panic also evident in his voice.

However, her horse had other ideas as it drove her away from his reach.

The loud rumble of thunder and the darkening of the sky wasn't helping her terrified state.

Infuriated and worried for her safety, Wade increased his pace, galloping after her.

He finally caught up with her breathing heavily.

He grabbed a piece of her horse's mane in one hand and used the other hand to give sharp tugs on the rein until

the horse slowed down and Kylie let out a breath she didn't
know she was holding.

The horse was now moving at a steadier rate.

He held her reins and led them to a narrow bush part
where he stopped them.

He dropped off his horse like it was nothing and went
closer to her.

"Let me help you down the horse."

"No, thank you, I can get down on my own." She tried
to get down by herself but had some trouble. She muttered a
curse-word under her breath feeling embarrassed.

He shook his head in amusement and held her by the
waist bringing her down without much trouble.

"You should really do something about that pride of
yours." He commented.

"Thanks,"

He raised his eyebrow still smiling "Thanks for the
advice or for saving your life?"

She couldn't help but smile back "For saving my life."

He found himself entranced by her beauty. That smile
that always made him yield to her wishes still worked on
him.

His eyes flicked down her body noting the typical
short white and blue dress she wore with a brown belt
around the waist matched with brown cowgirl boots.

And for some reason, she looked ridiculously
gorgeous in it. And for some stupid reason, he felt like taking
her in his arms and having his way with her. Showering her
with the desire, she had deprived him years ago and making
her yell his name, several times in the throes of pleasure just
like the old times.

Feeling nervous under his intense gaze, she cleared her throat drawing his attention back to her face.

He didn't even seem bothered by the fact that he had been caught checking her out fueling her anger.

''You know, for a married man, you do have some guts checking another woman out.''

He chuckled lightly. He was enjoying this too much and he loved that the misconception was riling her up.

''Well aren't you such a hypocrite, I caught you checking me out too.''

That shut her up and he smiled proudly ''Ride with me on my horse and I will take you back home.''

Her eyes widened at the impropriety of his suggestion ''I can't ride with a married man, it's improper.''

He scoffed seemingly impatient ''Common that's ridiculous, we have a lot to talk about especially about the Ranch's management and you can't keep running away from me like a child.''

''A child? I am simply being reasonable unlike you, chasing after a woman when you are married.''

He let out a laugh devoid of mirth ''I only chased after you to talk to you, would you have preferred that I let you die.''

''I would have preferred that you left me alone. I just want a little moment to myself, is that too much  to ask for.''

''If that's what you want,'' He resigned infuriated by her stubbornness.

He went back to his horse but was distracted by the sudden outpour of rain.

''Shit!'' He cursed under his breath.

''Why does everything have to work against my favour today?'' she complained as she embraced herself, shivering from the cold.

''We need to find shelter for the horses.''

She gave him an incredulous look ''Seriously, you are just worried about the horses, what about us?'''

He rolled his eyes and held unto the two horses ''If you know what's best for you, you will follow me or risk catching a cold in the rain.''

He started walking off taking the two horses with him.

''Where are you going?'' She asked still embracing herself.

He didn't answer or acknowledged her. He just kept on walking into the bushes.

She shook her head at his audacity. For her safety, she followed behind him until he stopped in front of an old, abandoned building.

It was the same old building where they used to sneak off to as kids when playing hide and seek. It was also the same building, where they had confessed their love, and shared their first kiss.

He led the horses into the dark building while she followed him inside.

The building was surprisingly clean with a fireplace which it didn't have before.

She wondered when it had been created.

Wade led the horses to the straw area and went back to meet Kylie who was busy trying to dry her blonde hair.

She looked like a goddess with her hair swept to the side looking ethereal in the dim lit room.

He willed his sinful thoughts away and went on setting the fireplace. He found two stones and after trying several times, he was able to light the fire.

He smiled at his achievement and stepped back.

She happily walked closer to the fireplace and sat down on the straw heaving a sigh at the much-needed warmness.

He sat down in front of her. Her dress had ridden up a little giving him an eyeful of her smooth thighs making him a little lightheaded.

The dress clung to her body like it was made for her specifically and it didn't help matters that it was now transparent and he could see through it and make out her black thong; A fact that she wasn't aware of.

He quickly looked way, looking at anything else but her for his own sanity.

''You have made a name for yourself and achieved everything you wanted to and more.'' She said her mind knowing that she might not have the chance to anymore.

He turned back to meet her eyes seeing the sincerity in them.

''But without you beside me,''

His eyes held a pain in them that reflected in hers.

''You have a beautiful family now.'' She ignored the pain she felt as she said those words.

''That's what you think.''

''What are you driving at?''

He seemed angry ''Don't you have any questions pending about me because I have a lot to ask you?''

''There's no point bringing back the past, Wade.''

"I have many questions Kylie, a lot that you have to answer and you can't keep giving me vague answers." He moved closer to you leaving you no breathing space.

"What do you want to know?"

"Did you ever miss me at all?" His voice highlighted his hurt.

What could she tell him? That till now he was still the only man she craved for. The only man that had made her feel like a woman in every way and the fact that him being so close to her was making her lightheaded. But it all felt pointless given the fact that he's married.

"Don't do this, Wade." She pleaded not finding it in her to lie as usual.

He held unto her arm "That doesn't answer my question." His voice was stern catching her off-guard.

Being this close to her and her glossy enticing lips was doing things to his body and against his better judgment; Wade listened to his heart and gave in to his inner desires.

He kissed her marveling at how soft her lips were. She seemed shocked at first but soon melted into the kiss.

She didn't have the will power to stop him nor did she want to.

She tasted amazing like Vanilla and he moaned as their tongue danced together in perfect rhythm.

He groaned and pulled her unto his lap. Her hand snaked round his neck and she caressed his hair feeling high on the kiss.

Feeling him harden under her, she felt herself get wet.

She grinded on him as he gripped her hips, groaning in pleasure.

He thrusted his hips forward hitting her at the right spot. She broke the kiss for air and met his half-lidded eyes filled with so much desire for her that sent her senses into overdrive.

He laid her on the bed of straws with her legs wrapped around his waist, with him on top of her.

Trailing kisses down her neck, he cupped her clad breasts, fondling and caressing them turning her into a moaning mess.

She had lost her train of thoughts. All she wanted was for him to touch her like she had craved all those years she had spent away from him.

The smell of his after shave and his cologne was intoxicating and the way his bulge pressed against her clad core made it throb aching to be touched.

As if he heard her thoughts, his hand slipped down her dress and up her thighs until he reached her clad core. He rubbed it earning a moan of pleasure from her.

He smirked against her neck "You are so wet."

He raised her dress up over her head and she assisted him in removing her bra.

He stared in awe at her full breasts. She had filled up nicely.

"You are so gorgeous."

She smiled proudly due to his compliment. He sucked on her breasts, taking turns and nibbling on them. She arched her back so he could get more of her.

In one swift movement, he slid her thong down and slid his finger in her, going deeper and stroking.

"Wade!" she said his name weakly.

He trailed kisses down her stomach still fingering her as she writhed under him.

He soon replaced his finger with his tongue, sucking her clean and giving her the pleasure she deserved.

He devoured every part of her, savoring her exquisite taste. His finger vigorously rubbed her as his tongue continued its ministration on her inner channel.

Her moans dissolved into breathless lusty sobs as she felt her insides clench and he sucked her orgasm off greedily.

Breathless but desperate for his touch, she helped him out of his shirt and unzipped his trousers leaving him in his black briefs.

He slid it down and she marveled at his perfectly defined muscled body.

He settled between her legs rubbing his hardness against her sending her whole body on fire.

Then it finally hit her. He had cheated on his wife with her and her stupid ass had allowed it, falling like jelly in his arms as he kissed her. Just as she tried to muster up all her strength to push him off her, he had slid in her making her lose her train of thoughts again.

He groaned  marveling at how tight she was.

He went slow at first allowing her to adjust to his enormous size before he began pumping into her harder and faster, going deeper and deeper.

He captured her lips letting her taste herself from his lips.

She grinded her core against his rhythmic thrusts while he sucked on her breasts.

"You feel so good." He growled as he deepened his thrusts with an almost vicious force.

She arched her back and wrapped her hands round him, rocking against him.

"That's my girl." He smiled

Feeling her orgasm building, he whispered in her neck "Let it go."

"Wade!" she wailed, her voice quavering and her inner channel gripping his cock.

His real undoing was seeing her orgasm, his cock pulsated just beneath her belly.

He continued to thrust into her until he expelled every drop of his cream in her.

He stilled buried deep in her, he closed his eyes savoring the thrilling effect of their joining.

Spent and afraid to crush her, he slowly slid out of her and laid next to her.

He pulled her into his arms and kissed her neck.

She felt tears spring up to her eyes as the gravity of what they had done caught up to her.

"This shouldn't have happened." She sobbed and pulled away from his arms.

"This was wrong, totally wrong. It should never have happened."

She got up and started to dress up while he sat up not quite getting her point.

"What are you talking about?"

She gave him an incredulous stare. He didn't seem fazed that he had cheated on his wife with her.

She wondered if he did it often and she was just one of his many escapades. She brushed the thought away feeling sick to her stomach.

She never in her wildest dream imagined that she would be a mistress. She always loathed those kind of women and alas, she had ended up just like them.

He was now standing in all his naked glory reaching for her but she took a step back.

"Please wear your clothes."

''Why are you acting like this?'' he asked as he wore his briefs.

''This was a mistake.'' With that being said, she ran out thanking her stars that the rain had stopped.

Wade stared at her retreating back and felt the urge to run after her but he didn't as he felt used.

She had just used him just like she had confessed twelve years ago

***

Sixteen-year-old, Wade panted as he ran towards the moving jeep of the ruthless Rhye Collins. He couldn't care less about what the man would do to him, he just wanted to talk to his sweetheart.

''Kylie!'' He shouted and she turned towards the car window and saw him.

She motioned to the driver to stop the car and the latter did while she got down from the car looking as beautiful as ever.

She frowned and folded her arms

''What do you want?''

He was too caught up with wanting to see her that he had missed the coldness in her voice.

''I came to see you. Frank told me that you are leaving for the states and I fought him over it. It isn't true right?'' He asked feeling a tinge of fear in his heart.

His love couldn't do that to him. She wouldn't leave him, he was sure of it.

She looked away from him for a second and turned towards the car to meet the cold glare of her uncle.

She sighed and turned back to look at him, her eyes devoid of emotions ''it's true.''

''And you didn't tell me?'' He couldn't believe that she would keep such a thing from him. Whatever happened to their oath of not keeping things away from each other.

''Why would I tell you?''

''Did he force you to do this?'' he referred to her uncle who was watching them through the window.

Usually the man would have dragged him off his ranch but he seemed strangely quiet that day.

''Nobody forced me into anything. It was my sole decision to move to the states.''

''But you didn't tell me anything.''

''Who do you think you are?''

He was taken aback by her question and touched her arm

''Kylie, why are you acting so cold? It's me, Wade, your boyfriend.''

She chuckled mirthlessly catching him off guard.

''You must be delusional. I never considered you as anything to me. I just used you to pass time.''

He shook his head vigorously not believing her one bit. It was too much  for his teenage heart to take.

''No, no you don't mean that.''

''I mean every word of what I said. I only used you and you are stupid to think that a poor worker like you, could have a chance with me.''

''Why are you doing this to me.'' He was on the edge of breaking down. It was taking every will power in him not to.

''Please cut out the drama and leave me alone. It would be for your own good if we just pretend that we don't know each other for the rest of our life.''

She turned her back to him and started to walk towards the car but he held her hand which she brushed away to his dismay.

''Don't touch me.'' With that being said, she entered the car.

He stood there and watched as the car zoomed off without her glancing back at him.

Then the guards carried him out of the ranch and dumped him in the bush.

***

She had trampled on his heart that day, made him feel used and humiliated him and yet he still loved her.

He quickly wore his cloth and mentally berated himself for following his heart and sleeping with her.

Chapter 8

Kylie ran as fast as her legs could carry her mentally berating herself for acting like a slut and sleeping with a married man.

As she ran past, the passers-by stared at her weirdly.

She knew she looked crazy with her wild hair and disheveled clothing but she didn't care.

She didn't slow down when she got to her ranch either. She just ran in brushing past a worried Sara and finally sinking down on the floor.

Sara walked in to see Kylie seated on the floor of her room with her back against the bed post.

''I was just about to set out to look for you. Are you ok? You keep on scaring me with your behavior these days, little one.''

She knelt in front of her and took note of her disheveled state.

''What happened to you?''

Kylie looked up to meet Sara's worried eyes ''You are going to hate me.''

Sara gave her an incredulous look ''Me, hate you? I could never. Just tell me what happened and I will help solve it.''

She broke into sobs and the fear in Sara's heart spiked. She raised Kylie by the chin to face her.

''Look at me, Kylie. I could never hate you. I may get mad but I could never hate you, so tell me what happened to you.''

Kylie took a moment to calm herself down before confessing ''I-I...I Slept with a married man.''

Sara couldn't believe her ears. It wasn't possible. Her little one couldn't possibly do such a thing.

''I didn't plan on doing it but one thing led to another and Wade kissed me and then everything happened in a flash, I wasn't thinking and-''

''Wait'' Sara cut her off.

''You mean you slept with Wade?''

Kylie nodded amidst sobs ''Yes, I didn't plan it.it just happened. I know you are disgusted with me.''

''But Wade is not married.''

Kylie's ears picked up at that ''What!''

Sara nodded smiling ''Wade is not married.''

''Then who is the woman staying at his ranch with her daughter, the little girl calls him daddy?''

Sara smiled ''She's his cousin, a widow. She had been staying at his ranch for at least four years now and the little girl has been calling him daddy since he's the only father figure she has.'' She explained to a perplexed Kylie.

''But why didn't he correct me when I thought he was married.''

''He was surely pulling your legs.''

She face-palmed herself.

''Oh my God! I feel so stupid and to top it all up, I left him and called what we had a mistake because of my misconception. How foolish of me?''

Kylie stood up startling Sara

''What are you up to?''

''I have to go back and apologize. I made him feel like nothing again and he's going to resent me the more for that.''

''No, you are not going in this state. Have you seen yourself in the mirror?''

Sara took her to stand by the tall, large mirror in the room and Kylie gasped in shock at her appearance. She looked like a mad woman who had just ran a marathon, the latter wasn't far from the truth.

''You are right. I really need a bath''

''Yeah you do.'' Sara chuckled and playfully pushed Kylie to the bathroom to freshen up.

Wade had just had a quick shower and headed to his kitchen for a much needed drink.

He opened his fridge and grabbed a bottle of brandy from there.

He popped the bottle open and gulped the content willing himself to forget the events of that day.

He felt so stupid letting his guard down and having his heart be broken for the second time by that darn woman who drove him insane.

Katherine stepped into the kitchen and frowned on seeing her cousin at his usual spot in the kitchen.

She had never been fond of his drinking but over the years she had learned that it was his coping mechanism.

''I 'm guessing you had a bad day.'' She pointed at the bottle in his hand.

He placed the bottle carelessly on the table ''Yes.''

''Easy on the drink, I have a letter for you from Sara.''

He frowned ''Sara?''

''Yeah, she told me to give you this and said that it's a must you read it.''

Despite himself, Wade smiled and collected the letter. Sara was one of the few people who loved him when he was still poor and she had always supported his relationship with Kylie even at the verge of losing her job.

Katherine excused herself while he opened the letter and read the content.

''If you are reading this that means I have passed. I don't deserve your sympathy neither do I deserve your forgiveness. I'm just writing this letter to rewrite my mistake. I had already ruined my sister's life. I don't want to ruin my niece's life any further.

Wade, if you are reading this, I want you to know that Kylie didn't break up with you on her own free will. I forced her to do it.

I threatened to kill you if she didn't pack up to the states and break up with you. She only broke up with you to save your life.

Even after moving over there, she wrote letters hoping that her Nanny would deliver them to you but I caught her one day and burnt those letters.

In fear for her Nanny's life and job, she stopped writing the letters and stopped communicating altogether.

I'm writing this now because I know that after my death, Kylie would come back to the Ranch.

I know you are still mad at her but deep down, you still are in love with her which is why you didn't strip me of my wealth when you had every right to do so.

If you are to be angry at anyone, let it be me because I ruined your love.''

Wade felt different kinds of emotions as he read the letter.

Curiosity at first, then anger that Rhye even had the audacity to write to him, then fury at the fact that he had misdirected his anger and hate to the wrong person, when it was Rhye that was at fault.

There was no more time to wait. He has to win his love back before it's too late.

He dashed out of his house ignoring the worried calls of his cousin.

Chapter 9

''Wade, this is a pleasant surprise.'' Sara smiled when she saw an impatient wade standing at the doorstep.

''I got your letter.'' He looked behind her, his eyes searching for kylie ''Where is She?''

Sara held unto his hand ''Come let me take you to her room so you two can talk.''

She followed Sara has she led him through the hallway to Kylie's room. Everything about the house still remained the same except for a few changes.

Kylie was standing by her mirror adjusting her flowery dress. Sara opened the door and pushed Wade in, gave him a thumbs up and excused herself.

''Sara, how do I look?'' she asked thinking it was Sara who had stepped into her room.

''Absolutely beautiful'' Wade replied.

She froze on hearing his voice behind her.

It had to be a dream. It just had to be. She looked behind her to see Wade beaming at her.

''Wade?''

''In flesh.'' He walked towards her staring at her with lovesick eyes. He had wasted twelve years hating the woman he loved and it was all for nothing because he never even hated her in the first place.

''Wade I-''

He put his finger on her lips cutting her off ''Shh- I know the truth now.''

She furrowed her eyebrow in confusion ''You know the truth?''

He nodded ''Yes, your uncle wrote this letter to me.''

He handed her the letter. She quickly opened it and frowned at the horrible handwriting.

She read the contents feeling vindicated.

Her uncle had done something right after all.

He wiped the stray tears from her eyes away ''I'm sorry.''

''I'm sorry too.'' Her voice broke.

''I wasted time hating you when I should have been thanking you for saving my life.''

She cupped his cheek, leaning her forehead against his ''How could you have known?''

''I'm sorry for leaving you, I thought you were married.''

He chuckled ''I get it.''

He planted a quick kiss on her lips ''I love you.''

The sincerity behind his words melted her heart and disposed of all her doubts away.

''I love you too, my cowboy.''

**THE END**

www.ingramcontent.com/pod-product-compliance
Lightning Source LLC
Chambersburg PA
CBHW020942160726
47993CB00007B/2895